The Snowman™

THE BOOK OF THE CLASSIC FILM

Based on the story by Raymond Briggs

Pictures from the animated film *The Snowman*

PUFFIN

The snow fell all night long.

When James woke up, he couldn't believe his eyes.

He leapt out of bed and rushed to the window. Outside, the world had turned a brilliant, glistening white.

Quickly, he tugged on his clothes and ran downstairs.

"Don't forget your boots!" Mum said.

James had never seen
so much snow!

He played for hours,
stamping up and down
the garden.

Then he started
to roll a snowball,

and it got bigger
and bigger!

Soon it was so big that it
gave James a brilliant idea . . .
He would make a snowman!

Carefully, he
built the body,

then rolled another ball for the head.

James ran inside
and found a tangerine
for the nose,

two pieces of coal for
eyes, an old green hat
and a matching scarf.

Last of all, James gave his snowman a great big smile.

He was perfect!

"Time for dinner!"
Dad called.

All evening, James sat by the window
so that he could gaze at his wonderful Snowman.

He would have stayed there all night,
but it was soon time for bed.

As he brushed his teeth, James
took one last look at his Snowman.

He snuggled down in bed.
"I hope he's still there in the morning,"
he thought, and he drifted off to sleep.

In the middle of the night,
James woke up and he
remembered his Snowman.

He crept downstairs.

As he looked out
at his Snowman . . .

. . . the most magical thing happened.

The Snowman came to life!

James shook the
Snowman's hand.

"Come in," he said.
"I'll show you around."

"In here," whispered
James, opening the
living-room door.

The Snowman loved the
Christmas tree, but thought
the fire was too hot!

So James took him to
the fridge to cool down.

Then they explored
the rest of the house,
and *even* tiptoed into
Mum and Dad's room . . .

. . . and tried on Dad's clothes!

"Perhaps we'd better go back outside," said James.

When they reached the garden, the Snowman
grabbed James's hand and started to run . . .

. . . faster and faster until . . .

... they were flying!

From all around, they were joined by flying snowmen.

Together, they flew over the city . . .

. . . out to sea . . .

. . . and on and on.

Until, at last, they landed at the North Pole.

The Snowman led James through the trees,
towards a clearing. James couldn't believe his eyes!

A large circle of snowmen were gathered,

and in the middle there was . . .

. . . Father Christmas!

"Just in time," smiled
Father Christmas.
"The party is about
to start!"

And what a party it was!

James and the Snowman danced all night long.

As the first rays of sunlight
appeared over the hills, Father
Christmas handed James a parcel.
"For me?" James gasped.

It was a soft blue scarf,
beautifully decorated
with snowmen.
"Oh, thank you!" cried James.

He gave Father Christmas a big hug.
And then it was time to go.

James and the Snowman soared into the air
and flew towards home.

When they arrived, it was nearly morning
and time for James to go back to bed.

James didn't want to leave his friend,
but he knew it was time to say goodbye.

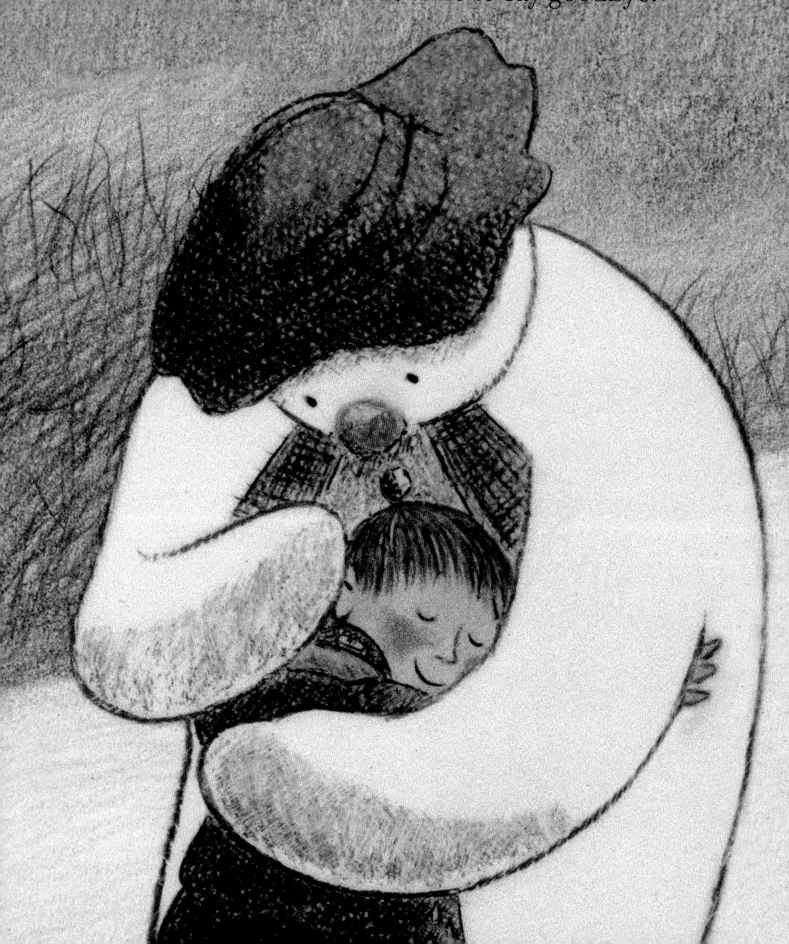

With one last look at the Snowman,
James went inside

and upstairs to bed.

Happy and exhausted, he fell asleep.

In the morning, James's first
thought was of the Snowman.

He jumped out of bed
and raced down the stairs,

past Mum and Dad . . .

. . . out of the door,

and into the garden.

But the Snowman had gone.